Today Is Valentine's Day!

Written and illustrated by

P.K. Hallinan

For two of my favorite Valentines,
Pam Ryan and Jerry Pallotta

Ideals Children's Books • Nashville, Tennessee
an imprint of Hambleton-Hill Publishing, Inc.

Published by Ideals Children's Books
An imprint of Hambleton-Hill Publishing, Inc.
Nashville, Tennessee 37218

Printed and bound in the United States of America

ISBN 1-57102-014-4

It's Valentine's Day
and there's love in the air!
What a wonderful chance
to show someone you care!

And isn't it lucky
you took enough time
to make every classmate
a great Valentine?

You colored with crayons—
cut paper apart—
till each card resembled
a Valentine heart.

Then you thoughtfully wrote
every classmate a note.

But hurry, you're late
and your hair is a muss!
Put your cards in a sack,
for here comes the bus!

Now don't show your friends
what you have in that sack!
Just tell them you're toting
a rather large snack.

And if they smile at you—
well, they're toting sacks too!

At school all the children
run every which way.
Red, white, and pink
are the colors today.

Once in your classroom,
excitement just grows,
and somebody's given
the teacher a rose!

No doubt it was Pruitt;
Jill dared him to do it.

On each student's desk
is a small cardboard box
just perfect for Valentines—
some even have locks.

When your teacher announces
it's time now to share,
you start dropping cards
in the boxes with care.

And when you're all done,
every classmate has one.

At recess you race
to a warm sunny spot,
and open your valentines
to see what you got.

And oh, what a haul!
What a great card from Paul!
And what a neat drawing
with cupids and all!

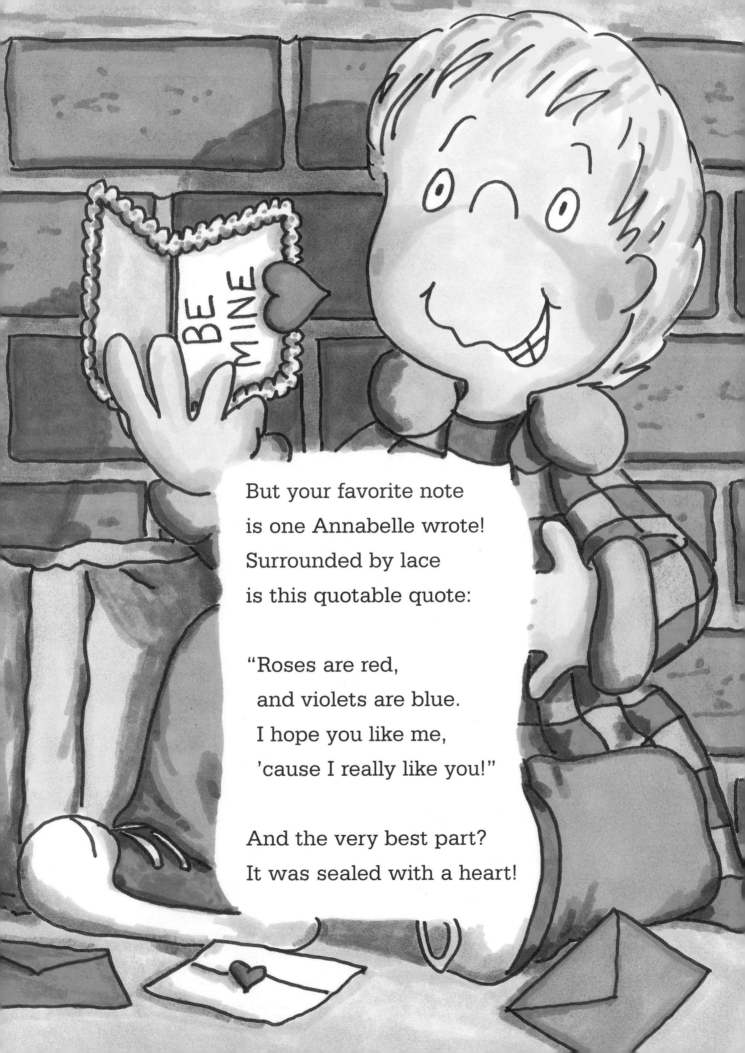

But your favorite note
is one Annabelle wrote!
Surrounded by lace
is this quotable quote:

"Roses are red,
  and violets are blue.
  I hope you like me,
  'cause I really like you!"

And the very best part?
It was sealed with a heart!

Back in the classroom
are two more surprises:
cookies and cupcakes
in all shapes and sizes!

The snacks are delicious—
it's all you can do
to laugh with your friends
as you're trying to chew.

Still you manage to eat
every goody and treat.

The clock ticks away
and the afternoon passes
like a bumblebee stuck
in a jar of molasses.

But the bell finally rings
so you scoop up your sack,
and you race to the bus
for the bumpy ride back.

Then you slowly spend time
reading each Valentine.

At home, you go flying
through the door like a bat,
and you race up the stairs
just as quick as a cat.

There's one final Valentine
yet to be done,
and you've got to make sure
it's the very best one.

So you draw a red heart
with an arrow and all,
then pick up your pencil
and let the words fall.

And when it's complete,
it's especially sweet.

"Dear best friend of mine,
I'd like you to know
that I cherish you more
than I'm able to show.

"Happy Valentine's Day!"